Sheep Dog

Sheep Dog

Words and photographs by George Ancona

Lothrop, Lee & Shepard Books • New York

*The dog shown on the title page and jacket
is a Great Pyrenees.*

Library of Congress Cataloging in Publication Data. Ancona, George.
Sheepdog. Summary: Describes the various breeds of dogs used to guard
and herd sheep, explains how they work, and discusses the importance of
these dogs to the sheep industry. 1. Sheep dogs—Juvenile literature.
[1. Sheep dogs. 2. Working dogs. 3. Dogs. 4. Sheep ranches] I. Title.
SF428.6.A53 1985   636.7'3   84-20100   ISBN 0-688-04118-3
ISBN 0-688-04119-1 (lib. bdg.)

To Carlos Carvalhosa

---

and to those who strive to
live in harmony
with nature.

heep graze calmly on open pasture, with young lambs following close to mother ewes. This peaceful scene is common to many farms and ranches across the United States.

A hungry coyote watches the flock from the surrounding woods. It picks out a lamb and begins to approach it.

The lamb, suddenly aware of the intruder, bleats a warning.

Panic seizes the flock and the sheep bolt away. The lamb desperately tries to keep up with its mother, but falls behind. The coyote swiftly overtakes the lamb. The predator lunges, clamps its teeth into the lamb's neck, and brings it to the ground. In a few seconds the lamb is dead.

Close by, the coyote's cubs have watched the kill. Their mother has just given them a lesson in hunting, as well as provided them with a meal.

When ranchers discover the remains of lambs killed by wild animals, they are often filled with rage. A dead lamb is a financial loss. Selling sheep for meat and wool is the way ranchers provide for themselves and their families.

All carnivores—animals that eat meat—are predators, including humans. Thousands of years ago people discovered ways to provide themselves with a constant food supply. They domesticated animals and became farmers. As they cleared the forests and pushed the wilderness back, they had to protect their flocks from the wild predators that roamed the forests. Even today, farmers and ranchers wage war on predators—wild hogs, bears, bobcats, cougars, eagles, wolves, foxes, wild dogs, and coyotes. For sheep ranchers, coyotes are the most damaging of these predators, mainly because the coyote population is so large. But the coyote, like the black bear, is not exclusively a carnivore. It also eats plants and berries in addition to mice and other small animals. This means that cougars and other members of the cat family would, if their numbers were larger, pose a greater threat than the coyote—for they eat only meat.

Government hunters and trappers help farmers control predators. Coyotes are trapped and killed. Sometimes a coyote will escape a trap by chewing off its foot. Unfortunately, animals that are not dangerous predators are also caught and crippled by the traps. Endangered species, such as grizzly bears, are captured and released in more remote areas.

Compound 1080, a poison that was once a great threat to coyotes and other members of the dog family (canids), has been banned by the federal government because it also kills other animals. Ecologists and others who are concerned about the welfare of the environment are against the use of these poisons. Scavengers that eat the dead

Traps, poison, and guns are typical predator control in the United States.

predators spread the poison into the food chain, which can eventually reach human beings. And predators such as the coyote are also needed to control rodent populations. But some ranchers who want the coyote exterminated are pressuring the government to once again legalize the use of Compound 1080.

Coyotes in captivity for study.

At the U.S. Sheep Experiment Station in Duboise, Idaho, coyotes are captured, bred, and raised in order to study their behavior. This research may lead to solutions for controlling the population of the species.

But the coyote is a very adaptable creature. Depending on conditions, the coyote can increase the size of its litter from four to ten pups. Scientists have determined that even if 90 percent of all the coyotes were killed, it would still take eighty years to eliminate the species. It seems clear that we need a better way to protect sheep from coyotes and other predators.

A common fate of coyotes in sheep country.

The people who look after the sheep and move them from one pasture to another are called herders or shepherds. It is a lonely life. High up on summer mountain pastures a shepherd lives with a flock of sheep, and has only a horse, a few dogs, and a rifle for company. Every three days a camp tender visits the shepherd and brings food, mail, and supplies.

Each morning the shepherd moves the flock to lower pastures to graze. At night, the sheep bed down on higher ground. When the flock is moved away from the main camp, the shepherd will sleep near them in a small tepee. Day in, day out, the shepherd's constant companion is the small herding sheep dog.

All dogs share the predatory legacy of their wild ancestors. In a herding dog the chase-and-bite instinct is controlled by training and the shepherd's commands. By shouts, whistles, and pointing the crook (the herding staff), the shepherd directs the dog to move the flock. Herding dogs move sheep by "eyeing" them with the same stalk that a predator uses. The "eye" is a signal to the sheep that means, "If you don't move, I'll bite you!" Herding dogs can also round up strays and find injured sheep. Without the shepherd to supervise them, though, herding dogs have been known to harass the sheep and even kill them.

A shepherd signals his Border collie, and the dog gives a ram "the eye."

Herding Dogs

The different breeds of dogs used for herding are divided into two types. One is the "heeler," which nips and barks at the heels of the animal. These are dogs like the Welsh corgi and the Australian cattle dog, who have pricked ears and long pointed noses. They are used primarily to herd cattle, because nipping behavior could damage sheep. The other type is the "header." Headers, such as the Border collie, run ahead of the sheep and cut them off. Headers often have higher crown-shaped heads than the heelers, and have "tulip" ears, which are halfway between floppy and pricked ears.

*An Australian cattle dog
(also known as Queensland blue heeler)
"heeling" a steer.*

A Border collie "heading" sheep.

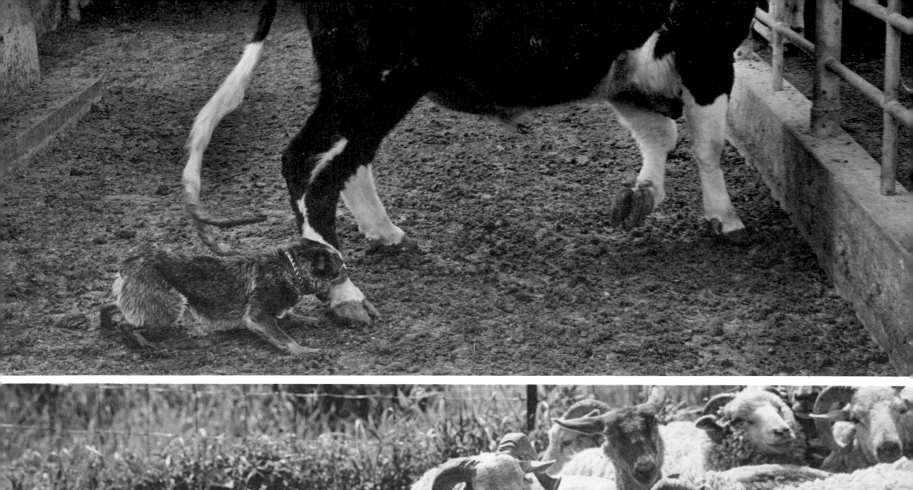

Herding Dogs

There are many breeds of herding dogs. The heeler and two headers shown here are typical examples. Note that the corgi does not have far to drop to the ground, which is one reason it is so successful as a heeler.

WELSH CORGI

The Welsh corgi was brought to Wales by the Central European Celts about 1200 B.C. They are used to herd cattle, and do so by biting the heels of cattle. This is why they are called "heelers." Corgis have very short legs and avoid being kicked because they are so close to the ground.

BORDER COLLIE

The Border collie is a header. Instinctively it can herd cattle, sheep, hogs, or poultry. Originating in England, it has been called the shepherd's collie, the English collie, the working collie, and the Border collie.

AUSTRALIAN KELPIE

The Australian kelpie works with sheep and is a header. Rather than nipping the sheep, it keeps them together by pushing them with its head and shoulders. Kelpies also do a good job looking after children.

This Great Pyrenees has deliberately placed itself between the flock and the photographer.

Raymond Coppinger

In their search for better ways to control predators, American scientists have looked overseas to regions where similar problems exist. In Central Europe and in the Near East, for example, wolves and bears prey on sheep, just as coyotes do in the United States. Researchers have studied the methods of sheepraising in these areas, and have found that shepherds use an ancient means of predator control. In addition to the herding dogs to control the livestock, particularly sheep, these herdsmen use another type of dog, the guard dog, to protect the flock against predators. These dogs, having been bred for their guarding instincts over thousands of years, need little or no training to protect sheep.

Lorna and Raymond Coppinger are biologists who went to Europe and the Near East in 1977 to study the behavior of working dogs. They saw cattle dogs in Switzerland and sheep dogs in Italy and France. In Yugoslavia they watched the legendary Shar Planinetz dogs as they plodded alongside flocks of sheep. Other guard dogs were observed in Italy, France, Hungary, Poland, and Turkey. All were big dogs with rounded heads, floppy ears, and a placid nature. But when strangers approached they were swiftly alert, placing themselves between the intruder and the flock. These guard dogs never chased sheep as herding dogs do. They related to sheep in ways almost unknown in the United States.

A guard dog is different from a herding dog in both behavior and appearance. Its loyalty is to the sheep instead of the shepherd. Wary of strangers and very independent, guard dogs can be left alone with the sheep. Many of the breeds even look like sheep: big, with shaggy coats. During the day they plod along with the grazing flock or loll in the shade. At night they are vigilant. They patrol the borders of the pasture, laying down a scent with their urine. In this way they make their presence known to any hunting predators.

A guard dog warns an intruder with a bark or a tense attack position with its tail curled up. It then retreats with its tail down, and gives a yelping bark. This confuses the predator. Then, without warning, the dog attacks. No 28-pound coyote will tangle with a 100-pound dog. And most coyotes and other predators prefer to obtain their meals without a fight.

It is believed that all breeds of European guard dogs have a common ancestry, since the mountain ranges where they work run together. Beginning in Portugal, the mountains extend along Europe's southern ranges to the Anatolian Plateau of Turkey and Iran. In each area the guarding instincts of the breeds developed in isolation. They were strengthened by the dogs' survival in these rugged terrains.

Both males and females are used as guard dogs. The dogs are big-boned; they stand about 30 inches at the shoulder, and weigh 75 to 100 pounds. They vary in color from very dark to white. The lighter colored dogs are better suited to work in the hot sun. Some have long thick coats that provide good insulation against heat, cold, and predators' teeth.

Europe and the Near and Middle East

MAP BY ISABEL ANCONA

Guard Dogs

GREAT PYRENEES

The Great Pyrenees is named for the mountains of its origin. The Pyrenees range divides France from Spain. It is believed that the breed descended from the Tibetan mastiff, a powerful, smooth-coated dog. Phoenician traders brought them by sea from Asia Minor, and the Aryan invaders brought them by land.

Fossils of the Great Pyrenees have been found dating back to 1800–1000 B.C. Fifteenth-century French writers tell of "the great dog of the mountains" that guarded the Chateau of Lourdes. By 1675 it was adopted as the royal dog of Louis XIV, the French king. Wearing spiked collars, the great dogs would patrol at night, guarding against the bears and wolves that roamed the mountains.

The male Pyrenees stands 27 to 32 inches high and weighs 100 to 125 pounds. As with all breeds, the female is slightly smaller. Both sexes are usually white with darker yellow splotches. They are among the gentler of the guard dog breeds, and were originally introduced in the United States as pets.

MAREMMA

The Maremma comes from Italy, from the Plains of Maremma and the Abruzzi Mountains. The breed has been used there to guard sheep for centuries. It is possible that the Great Pyrenees, the kuvasz of Hungary, and the Maremma all have a common ancestor, since they are so similar. All three breeds have long, thick, white coats, with the Maremma and the kuvasz having longer muzzles.

The Maremma tends to be friendlier than the dogs of the East. Perhaps this is because there are now fewer wolves in Italy to guard against. The Maremma is more suited to a smaller farm, where the dog has more contact with people.

Slightly smaller than the Great Pyrenees, a male Maremma stands 26 to 29 inches high and weighs 75 to 80 pounds.

KOMONDOR

The komondor is one of the oldest breeds of European guard dog. It has been a distinct breed for 1,000 years, and is of Tibetan ancestry. It is believed that in the thirteenth century, tribal families of Kuns (then in Turkey), emigrated with their sheep and dogs to Hungary. The name probably comes from *kunun-du*, meaning "belonging to the Kuns."

The long white coat of the komondor (plural—komondorak) hangs down to the ground in thick cords. These sturdy cords protect the dog from the mountain weather and from predators' teeth. The male komondor stands 26 to 32 inches high and weighs 80 to 100 pounds.

SHAR PLANINETZ

This sheep dog is found in the Shar Planina Mountains of Macedonia, in southern Yugoslavia. It is similar to the Great Pyrenees and the Maremma, but smaller. Although the color of this breed varies greatly, from white to black, most of these dogs are a warm brown color with a characteristic dark muzzle.

The Shar Planinetz will greet strangers with ferocious barking. If the Shar accepts the presence of a stranger, however, it will not show friendliness, but will move away and stand aloof.

KUVASZ

In the year 2250 B.C. the great Babylonian king Hammurabi inscribed a series of laws that mentioned two of the breeds now found in Hungary—the kuvasz and the komondor.

The kuvasz (plural—kuvaszok) has been bred by Hungarian herdsmen for 500 years. But the breed was used by herdsmen in Sumeria as far back as 8,000 years ago. *Ku,* the first syllable of the name of the breed, is from the Sumerian word for dog, *kudda.*

The word *assa* means horse. *Kuassa* meant a dog that guarded and ran alongside horses and horsemen. *Kuvasz* is the Hungarian version of the Sumerian word.

Kuvaszok were used not only to guard sheep and homes, but to hunt wolves and wild boar. This history explains the alert behavior of the breed. The dog is gentle with the people it lives with and is extremely protective of them. It stands about 28 to 30 inches high and weighs 95 to 100 pounds.

ANATOLIAN SHEPHERD

This strong, large-headed dog is a native of Turkey and of Asia Minor's Anatolian Plateau. It has guarded sheep in this rugged, isolated terrain for over 6,000 years. In Babylonian times the breed was used as a fighting dog in war, and for hunting lions and wild horses.

The dogs vary in appearance. They range from having shaggy to smooth coats in light or dark colors. The classic coloring is black ears and a black muzzle, with a tan smooth coat. Others are pure white.

Anatolians stand 29 inches high and can weigh as much as 150 pounds. Turkish shepherds crop the ears and tails of their dogs to prevent predators from grabbing them in a fight. Some shepherds add an iron-spiked collar as protection. The dogs are gentle with farm animals and family, but become aggressive with predators, human or animal. These dogs are used to working in large, uninhabited areas.

Raymond Coppinger introduces
a Maremma pup to sheep.

Raymond and Lorna Coppinger, on their scientific study overseas, saw for themselves how these different breeds of guard dogs work with flocks and herds. They decided to bring some European dogs back to the United States, to try to determine whether the dogs could guard livestock in this country. The biologists returned from their travels with eight puppies—four from Yugoslavia and four from Italy. In addition, they picked up six Border collie puppies in Scotland. This was the beginning of the Livestock Dog Project at Hampshire College in Amherst, Massachusetts. The big question of the research project was, "Since dogs themselves are predators, how can they guard sheep?"

Biologists understand that the behavior of animals is related to the way they are built. Wings are for flying, feet for walking. The anatomy and characteristics of a species are determined by the genes of the parents, which are passed on to their offspring. Animal breeders select two animals whose characteristics they value. These animals are then bred, and the desired characteristics are thereby strengthened in the offspring. In the Livestock Dog Project, the Coppingers have looked for those guarding instincts that will work well in protecting livestock in the United States. In addition to the instinct to guard, size is also important. A dog that can stand against a predator must be comparable in size and strength.

Newborn Border collie

Newborn Maremma

All animals of the canine family (wolves, dogs, foxes and coyotes) develop similarly. Almost all look alike at birth. They are born with their eyes closed, ears against their heads, and cannot smell. But they are able to suck and can find the teat of their mother. They stay together in the litter when their mother is away.

All pups mature in one or two years. Before they mature they go through a juvenile period. During this period their shape and behavior change, helping them to make the transition from the security of the den to the rigor of adult life. The Coppingers have divided this juvenile period into four stages.

A litter of Maremmas.

FIRST STAGE

During the first stage the pups begin to
loosen their contact with their mother, the
den, and their littermates by sitting outside
the den. In the wild they get food by licking
their mother's face, getting her to
regurgitate, and then fighting over the
food. Any strange intrusion sends them
scurrying back into the den, yelping, biting,
snarling, or crouching in fear.

Maremma pups responding to a cat's intrusion, just as would pups in the wild.

These Maremma pups are now old enough to be no longer startled by the unfamiliar.

SECOND STAGE

During the second stage all pups begin to play with objects. At first they play with each other or with their mother's tail. Later they begin to play with leaves, sticks, or insects.

An adult Border collie playing fetch.

Many of the dogs we keep as pets are breeds that tend to remain in the second stage in both behavior and appearance. They play with objects and chase balls almost all their lives. It is easy to train these dogs to perform tricks and specific tasks. Retrievers, hounds, and spaniels—with their floppy ears and broad heads—are especially puplike in appearance, and they almost never grow tired of chasing and retrieving objects.

Curly coated retrievers doing what they love best.

THIRD STAGE

At the third stage pups begin to "stalk." The "victim" may be imaginary, or it may be a sleeping littermate. The pounce is a stiff-legged action, like the pouncing of coyotes and wolves. If the victim moves, a short chase, or "heading off," may occur.

Here a Border collie pounces in the same way that the coyote does. Stage-three behavior may be an advantage to dogs that are needed to run ahead of cattle and head them off.

Coyote pouncing.

FOURTH STAGE

In the fourth stage pups learn to hunt by
watching their parents. When hunting, wild
canids, such as the coyote, concentrate on
the heels of the victim and bring it down by
biting through the rear leg muscle. This is
called *hamstringing*. After the pups go
through all four stages of development,
they too can then hunt and survive on their
own, just as their parents do.

Domestic dogs with stage-four behavior
are called "heelers." They are cattle-driving
dogs and look closest to wild dogs with their
long pointed noses and pricked ears.

*The herding dog's ears, opposite page, are similar
to the coyote's.*

This Maremma pup licks a sheep as it would its mother.

(Opposite page) The young Maremma in the background will learn quickly from its adult "supervisor."

The behavior of European guard dogs does not seem to go beyond stage two. As pups they play with each other, but ignore sticks and balls. As adults, they still look like puppies with their short muzzles, rounded heads, and floppy ears. They relate to sheep as if they were littermates, licking their faces as they once did their mothers'. When a predator approaches, the guard dogs get between the flock and the intruder and bark. Should the predator remain, it is subject to a short, snarling attack.

Even when herding dogs and guard dogs are raised together in the same pen, they develop differently. Herding dogs are quick to respond to commands; guard dogs are slower. Herding dogs develop the "eye," which is the tendency to watch potential prey eagerly, then follow with stalking behavior, before pouncing. Guard dogs never develop the eye, or stalk. As the guard dogs grow larger than the herding dogs, they slow up and tend to keep to themselves. They don't respond to objects thrown to them, and they prefer sheep to people.

The Livestock Dog Project at Hampshire College has been placing European guard dogs with American sheep farmers since 1978. When pups are about ten weeks old they are taken to farms and ranches around the country. They need little or no special training and know instinctively what to do when placed with the sheep.

Cooperating ranchers introduce the pup into their flock and the bonding process begins—the sheep must learn to accept the dog as a protector and not as a threat. Through the bonding process, the guard dog develops loyalty to the sheep. Contact with people is discouraged. The pups begin to work when they are six months old, but it takes two years for them to mature and to be trusted alone with the sheep. A rancher will often keep two young guard dogs on the range. It is better that they play together than with the sheep, which they might unintentionally injure.

Jay Lorenz, of the Livestock Dog Project, preparing to take guard pups out West.

Many factors determine the success or failure of a guard dog. A dog that performs poorly on one ranch may do better on another. Often the care and skill of the rancher determine how a dog will behave. Sometimes, for example, a rancher may feed a dog too close to the house. Then the dog leaves the flock unattended while it comes home to eat.

Cooperating farmers and ranchers send in reports on how the dogs perform to Jay Lorenz at the Livestock Dog Project. There, each dog's performance is stored in a computer. Dogs that perform well will be bred to improve future generations of guard dogs. Those that perform poorly or behave dangerously are not used for breeding and are retrained to serve a function for which they are better suited.

In addition to a dog's performance, the computer stores information about each ranch or farm, its pastures, the sheep, and how many sheep, if any, are killed by predators. Knowing these factors helps to determine what location would be best for a particular kind of dog.

Lorna Coppinger
analyzing a dog's performance.

Adapting European guard dogs to work in the United States is an experiment that is having positive results. Some breeds are better suited to a particular region than others. The larger, more aggressive dog works better on open rangeland. Smaller dogs are better on farms where more people come and go.

Dogs from Europe must adjust to the environment of the United States. They must learn to avoid traps. They must also learn to avoid animals like the porcupine, which does not exist in Europe. In the United States, unlike European countries, sheep are managed with a minimum of supervision. When faced with sheep spread out over a vast North American range, a good dog may become confused and perform poorly. It will be several years before it is known which dogs to use in which situations.

An Anatolian and a Great Pyrenees, both two years old, at the U.S. Experimental Sheep Station with their handler.

Up to recent years, shepherds in the United States have used only herding dogs to herd sheep. The shepherd will always need the herding dog, but, in addition, a guard dog can be an important partner. Even though a sheep rancher must invest two years of time and money waiting for a dog to mature, guard dogs are more humane and cheaper than traps or poison, more ecologically sensible, and are proving to be more effective in the battle against coyotes.

*This Great Pyrenees has
adapted well to its American home, and sends
a coyote running.*

ACKNOWLEDGMENTS

This book would not have been possible without the kind help, hospitality, and cooperation of Dr. Raymond Coppinger, Professor of Biology, of Lorna Coppinger, Faculty Associate in Biology, and of Research Assistant Jay Lorenz, all at the Livestock Dog Project at Hampshire College in Amherst, Massachusetts. They provided me with access to their dogs and sheep, and to their knowledge, research, and writings. Jay Lorenz's cooking was pretty fine, too. Out West, Roger Woodruff and Jeff Green of the U.S. Experimental Sheep Station at Dubois, Idaho provided me with much of the information needed to do this book. They also arranged for me to visit with the sheep herders and their flocks and dogs, and provided the coyotes that I photographed. Many thanks to them and to the many ranchers, farmers, and herders who took the time to teach me.

BIBLIOGRAPHY

Coppinger, Lorna, and Raymond Coppinger. "Livestock Guarding Dogs." *Country Journal,* April 1980, pp. 68–77

———. "Livestock Guarding Dogs." Livestock Dog Project, Hampshire College, Ma., 1978

———. "Livestock Guarding Dogs That Wear Sheep's Clothing." *Smithsonian,* April 1982, pp. 64–73

———. "So Firm a Friendship." *Natural History Magazine,* March 1980, pp. 12–77

———. "Protecting the Flock." *Sheep! Magazine,* July 1981, pp. 63–65

Davis, Henry P. *The New Dog Encyclopedia.* Stackpole Books, Harrisburg, Pa.

Green, Jeffery S. and Roger A. Woodruff. "Guarding Dog Economics." *Sheep! Magazine,* July 1981, pp. 18–19

Harned, Marilyn. "Anatolian Shepherd Dog: An Ancient Breed." *Rangelands,* April 1982, pp. 63–65

McLaughlin, John. *The Canine Clan.* Viking, New York, 1983

Nelson, David D., and Judith N. Nelson. "The Livestock Guarding Dogs of Turkey." *National Wool Grower,* September 1980

Unkelbach, Kurt. *The American Dog Book.* E.P. Dutton, New York, 1976

Wilt, Jan. "Our Incredible Komondor." *Countryside,* June 1980, pp. 37–39